W9-BJF-979

NO LONGER THE PROPERTY OF
BALDWIN PUBLIC LIBRARY

Nate the Great
and the
STOLEN BASE

Nate the Great
and the
STOLEN BASE

by Marjorie Weinman Sharmat

illustrations by Marc Simont

BALDWIN PUBLIC LIBRARY

A Yearling Book

Published by
Bantam Doubleday Dell Books for Young Readers
a division of
Bantam Doubleday Dell Publishing Group, Inc.
1540 Broadway
New York, New York 10036

If you purchased this book without a cover you should be aware that this book is stolen property. It was reported as "unsold and destroyed" to the publisher and neither the author nor the publisher has received any payment for this "stripped book."

Copyright © 1992 by Marjorie Weinman Sharmat
Illustrations copyright © 1992 by Marc Simont

All rights reserved. No part of this book may be reproduced or transmitted in any form or by any means, electronic or mechanical, including photocopying, recording, or by any information storage and retrieval system, without the written permission of the Publisher, except where permitted by law. For information address Coward McCann, Inc., a division of The Putnam & Grosset Group, 200 Madison Avenue, New York, N.Y. 10016.

The trademarks Yearling® and Dell® are registered in the U.S. Patent and Trademark Office and in other countries.

ISBN: 0-440-40932-2

Reprinted by arrangement with The Putnam & Grosset Group, on behalf of Coward McCann, Inc.

Printed in the United States of America

March 1994

27 26 25 24

4836283

For my father Nathan "Nate" Weinman
and with appreciation to all the Nathans everywhere
who feel a special bond with Nate the Great

I, Nate the Great, am a detective.
Sometimes I'm a baseball player.
This morning I was a detective
and a baseball player.
My dog, Sludge, and I
went to the field.
I had to practice batting
and running and fielding.
I belong to a team.

ROSAMOND'S RANGERS.
Rosamond, Annie, Harry,
Oliver, Esmeralda, Claude,
Finley and Pip belong, too.
They were at the field.
Rosamond's four cats were there.
They are the team's mascots.

Annie's dog Fang was there.

Fang is not on the team.

He is not a mascot.

Fang should have stayed home.

Rosamond came up to me.

"We can't practice today," she said.

"Somebody stole second base."

"We can get another second base,"
I said. I bent down
and picked up a big stone.

"A stone for second base?"
Rosamond said.

"Not while I'm coach.

Everybody uses stones.

Rosamond's Rangers do not."

Rosamond is a strange coach.

9

That was no surprise.

Rosamond is a strange person.

She said, "When we play

baseball, I bring first base.

Oliver brings second base.

And Annie brings third base."

Rosamond held up a

large tuna fish can.

"Here's today's first base.

Nobody stole it."

Annie held up a large dog bone.

"Here's today's third base," she said.

"Nobody ate it."

Fang and Sludge sniffed.

Oliver said,

"I was going to bring

the same base I brought yesterday.

But somebody stole it.

It was the best."

I, Nate the Great, did not think

Oliver's second base was the best.

It was an octopus

made of gloopy purple plastic.

Oliver collects eels.

He is saving up

for a real octopus.

"We need a detective to find

my second base," he said.

"Make another octopus," I said.

Oliver was mad.

"You think it's easy to make

those long, curling arms?" he said.

"Besides, that was

my good-luck octopus."

"Very well. I, Nate the Great,

will take the case."

I knew what Oliver's

octopus looked like.

It had eight long, curling arms.

It looked oozy and slimy.
"Where do you keep
your octopus?" I asked.
"On my bookcase," Oliver said.
"But when I went to get it
this morning, it wasn't there."
"We must go to your house," I said.
I wrote a note to my mother.

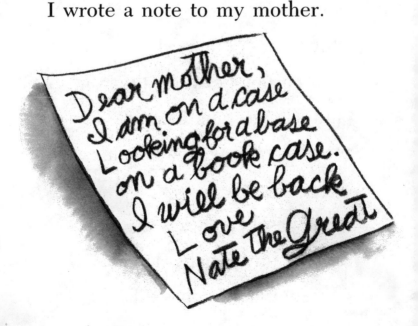

Dear mother,
I am on a case
Looking for a base
on a book case.
I will be back
Love
Nate the Great

I left the note at my house.

Then Sludge, Oliver and I

went to Oliver's house.

He lives next door.

He took us to his room.

I saw his bookcase.

It was full of books.

So far, so good.

But it was squeezed

in a corner between the wall

and a huge tank of eels.

And the top of it was a mess.

It was covered

with baseball things.

Cards, mitts, balls, and bats.

"I've got so much stuff

on my bookcase

that some of it falls

to the floor,"

Oliver said.

"But I pick it right up."

"This is a real mess," I said.

"Your octopus must
be hidden under something
on top of your bookcase."
I, Nate the Great,
moved things,
piled things,
and sorted things.
Sludge sniffed.
"I have just found
something important," I said.
"What?" Oliver asked.
"A telephone. It was hidden
under two baseball mitts.
And the cord is still hidden."
"The cord goes down the back
of the bookcase

and plugs into the wall,"
Oliver said.
"It's boring.
But the telephone is nice.
I like to call people."
"I know it," I said.
Oliver is a pest.
He follows people.
He calls people.

17

At last I said,

"I do not see the octopus

on your bookcase."

"So you can't find it either,"

Oliver said.

"*On* is only one place to look,"

I said. "*In* is another."

I looked in Oliver's eel tank.

"Your octopus did not fall

in there," I said.

"Perhaps it fell

down one side

of your bookcase."

"But my bookcase

is squeezed between

the eel tank on one side

and the wall on the other,"
Oliver said.
"I, Nate the Great,
need a flashlight."
Oliver gave me a flashlight.
I flashed the light down

both sides of the bookcase.

"The octopus did not slip through,"
I said.

"So you struck out," Oliver said.

"No. There is one more place
to look. Perhaps your octopus
fell down the *back*
of the bookcase."

"But you can't get
back there,"
Oliver said.

"No problem. I, Nate the Great,
can peer over the top."
I leaned forward.
"Ouch!"
I bumped my head.

"The wall is in the way,"
I said. "I can't see down."
I stretched out flat
on the floor
in front of the bookcase.
"Now what are you doing?"
Oliver asked.
"I am flashing the flashlight
toward the floor at the back
of your bookcase," I said.
I, Nate the Great,
saw something.

I reached for it
and pulled it out.
It was not the octopus.
It was a baseball card.
"So *that's* where my

Babe Ruth card went!"

Oliver said.

"I, Nate the Great, say

that your octopus did not fall

down the back of your bookcase."

I walked around the room.

I looked hard.

"I do not see the octopus

anywhere in this room,"

I said. "When was the last time

you saw it?"

Oliver shrugged. "I'm not sure.

When I got home

from the game yesterday,

I pulled it out

of my pocket

and dumped it on my bookcase

with my other baseball stuff."

"Then what?"

"Then I used my telephone.

I called everybody I know."

"I believe it," I said.

"Then I went out and
followed people
for the rest of the day."

"I believe that, too," I said.

"What did you do last night?"

"I slept," Oliver said.

I, Nate the Great,
was getting nowhere.

Oliver said, "This morning
when I went to get my octopus,
I couldn't find it."

"Has anyone else
been in this room?"
I asked.
"Only my eels," Oliver said.
"Then I, Nate the Great,

must go out and
look for clues."
"I will follow you,"
Oliver said.
"Stay by your telephone," I said.
Sludge and I went back
to the baseball field.
"The octopus was second base
in yesterday's game,"
I said to Sludge.

"Perhaps there's a clue here."
I saw Rosamond standing
under a tree with her cats.
"I just tossed my baseball mitt
into the air," she said.
"But it came down
on a branch of this tree
and it's stuck there."
I looked up.
I saw the mitt
on a branch.
"My cats can go up
and shake it down,"
Rosamond said.
"My cats are smart.
If Oliver's octopus

wasn't made of plastic,
they could find it.
An octopus is something
like a tuna fish, isn't it?"
I, Nate the Great,
did not want
to think about that.
I walked over
to where second base
had been.
I kicked the dirt around.
I saw something long
and curling
and oozy and slimy-looking.

It was one arm of Oliver's
octopus.
Oliver's octopus had eight arms.
I had found one.
I had solved one eighth
of this case.
"Look for more octopus arms,"
I said to Sludge.
Sludge and I walked
around the field.
Then Sludge ran ahead.
He sniffed.
He stopped.

He brought me another octopus arm.

"Good work, Sludge," I said.

We kept looking.

But we could not find

any more octopus arms.

Sludge and I went home.

We had to think about the case.

I made pancakes for myself.

I gave Sludge a bone.

"We are looking for
a purple plastic octopus
with six arms,"
I said. "Or maybe less.
When Oliver took
the octopus home
from the last game,
he dumped everything
on his bookcase.
He did not notice that

two arms were missing.

What else didn't he notice?"

I went to the telephone.

I called Oliver.

He answered right away.

"Who did you follow

before you went home

from yesterday's game?" I asked.

"Annie," he said.

"And your octopus was in

your pocket, right?"

"Right," Oliver said.

"Thank you," I said.

I hung up.

"We must go to Annie's house,"

I said to Sludge.

Annie was sitting in front
with Fang.
"I am looking for
octopus arms," I said.
I looked at Fang.
I did not want to do that.
"Your dog will eat almost anything,"
I said. "Like second base."

34

"Why would he eat
gloopy purple plastic?" Annie said.
She held up a dog bone.
"This is third base
and Fang didn't eat it.
I'm very proud of him."
Fang wagged his tail.
"But Fang isn't perfect,"
Annie said.
That was no surprise to me,
Nate the Great.
Fang stopped wagging.
Annie said, "When Oliver
followed me after the last game,
Fang followed Oliver.
I think Fang snatched

some of the octopus
from Oliver's pocket."

"Aha!" I said. "So second base
was stolen after all."

"Fang only took
one octopus arm,"
Annie said. "And here it is."
Annie handed a very dirty
octopus arm to me.

"I just found this
in my yard," she said.
"Fang buried it there."

"Did Oliver see the snatch?"
I asked.

"No," Annie said.
"He was too busy following me."

"So Oliver's octopus
is missing three arms
and maybe more,
and Oliver doesn't know it,"
I said.
I said good-bye to Annie.
"This case is as good as solved,"
I said to Sludge.
"All we need to find
are a few more octopus arms."
We went to Oliver's house.
Oliver was talking
on the telephone.

Oliver kept talking.

I knew what I must do:

Get down on the floor.

Reach under the bookcase.

And unplug the telephone

from the wall.

But when I had looked

under there for the octopus,

I did not see the plug
or the cord.
They must have been
too high up.
I had to think of something else.
"HANG UP!" I shouted.
It worked.
Oliver hung up.

I held up the three octopus arms.

"I, Nate the Great, found these.

The case is in good shape.

But your octopus is not."

"I know that," Oliver said.

"When I brought it home,

I saw that I had

a five-armed octopus

instead of eight."

"Why didn't you tell me?"

I asked.

Oliver smiled.

"What difference does that make

to an octopus?

Five are plenty."

It made a big difference

to me, Nate the Great.

I said, "Then I still have to find
a mostly together octopus."

"Right," Oliver said.

I said, "I, Nate the Great,
have struck out.
But I will be back."

Sludge and I went
to the field.

Rosamond and her cats
were gone.

Her mitt was gone
from the tree.

I sat down on a log.

Sludge sat beside me.

I thought about the case.

I had found a telephone,

a baseball card,

and octopus arms.

None of these mattered.

Or did they?

I looked up at the tree

where Rosamond's mitt

had been stuck.

Hmmm.

I thought about the telephone again.

And the octopus arms.

Those *long, curling* arms.

And I knew where the octopus

had to be!

Sludge and I ran back
to Oliver's house.
Oliver was talking
on the telephone.
I started to pull his bookcase
away from the wall.
Oliver hung up.
"I need to look

43

behind your bookcase," I said.
I, Nate the Great, pulled harder.
Then I peered behind the bookcase.
I saw the telephone cord
plugged into the wall.
And I saw something else.
Stuck on the cord,
with two of its arms
curled around it,
was a five-armed

purple plastic octopus.

The case was solved!

I reached in to grab the octopus.

R-I-P!

The octopus now had four arms.

But that was plenty.

I held up the octopus.

"You found second base!"

Oliver said. "But how

did you know it was there?"

"Your octopus's arms are long

and curling," I said.

"That makes it easy

for them to catch

onto something.

That was a clue.

But I didn't know it
until I thought
about Rosamond's mitt
that had caught
on a branch.
It fell there
after she tossed it.
It should have landed
on the ground.
When your octopus
fell off the back

46

of your bookcase,

it should have landed

on the floor.

That's where I looked.

But it never got there.

Because its arms were caught

on the telephone cord."

"Hooray!" Oliver said. "Now we

can have baseball practice.

I will call the team."

Oliver made his calls

while I pushed the bookcase back.

Then Oliver, Sludge and I

walked to the field.

I, Nate the Great,

went up to bat.

I looked around the field.

I saw first base.

A tuna fish can.

I saw second base.

Oliver's four-armed octopus.

Then I saw third base.

The dog bone was there.

In Fang's teeth.

Fang was third base.

I gripped the bat.

I, Nate the Great, hoped

I would strike out.